BLUFF

also by Danez Smith

[insert] boy
Don't Call Us Dead
Homie / My Nig

BLUFF

– poems –

Danez Smith

Chatto & Windus
LONDON

1 3 5 7 9 10 8 6 4 2

Chatto & Windus, an imprint of Vintage, is part of the Penguin Random House group
of companies whose addresses can be found at global.penguinrandomhouse.com

Penguin
Random House
UK

First published in the United States of America by Graywolf Press in 2024
First published in Great Britain by Chatto & Windus in 2024

Book design by Rachel Holscher

penguin.co.uk/vintage

Printed and bound in Great Britain by Clays Ltd, Elcograf S.p.A.

The authorised representative in the EEA is Penguin Random House Ireland,
Morrison Chambers, 32 Nassau Street, Dublin D02 YH68

A CIP catalogue record for this book is available from the British Library

ISBN 9781784745738

Penguin Random House is committed to a sustainable future
for our business, our readers and our planet. This book is made
from Forest Stewardship Council® certified paper.

contents

BLUFF

anti poetica

there is no poem greater than feeding someone
there is no poem wiser than kindness
there is no poem more important than being good to children
there is no poem outside love's violent potential for cruelty
there is no poem that ends grief but nurses it toward light
there is no poem that isn't jealous of song or murals or wings
there is no poem free from money's ruin
no poem in the capital nor the court
most policy rewords a devil's script
there is no poem in the law
there is no poem in the west
there is no poem in the north
poems only live south of something
meaning beneath & darkened & hot
there is no poem in the winter nor in whiteness
nor are there poems in the landlord's name
no poem to admonish the state
no poem with a key to the locks
no poem to free you

ars america (in the hold)

from the stars   if the stars   truly are that way back mother   if stars
then space & gas then water   & rock & bacteria   & fish & bird
& beast & us   if us   is from the stars   if the legacy of the stars
led to   if the lineage of the stars   led to the inspired cruelty on those ships
if the stars were born   &   the children of stars   birthed not only a language
but nations   but empires   & casualties of riches   & made an art of cruelty
if the babes of stars did that   those unspeakable yet done   devil blessed   those things
starved & bloodrotted   what language don't hold true enough   those things
worse than murder   slower   murder too kind a thing to say it was   murder better
than what the docks held   if the stars gave birth to that   kill the stars
kill the mother of stars   kill all reason   kill god
before he sets the ships into motion   when he calls the light alive

Warriors are poets and poems and all the loveliness here in the worlds.

     Amiri Baraka

Here ends civility
Now we know the strategy of stars

     June Jordan

                            I was born from an apocalypse
and have come to tell you what I know—

     Franny Choi

on knowledge

maury, i'm not the father of my
thoughts. the voice who say kill
yourself ain't got my nose, one
who say poetry over wartime
got one blue eye, all my family
got the same good yoke but
something peckish & not ours
say ka-chain! ka-chain! ka-ching!

i want to believe in my mind, but
that house went spliff back in '14.
year of new blood. year with ten
years & a fox inside. that year i
wanted to live. wanted us alive.
they gave me money to want to
live. i wanted more. i pulled the
dead from clouds for a come up.
tendered   violence.   tenderized
violence. god said *charge!* my life
heard *credit!* my career came on
an elegy's back. i made us media.
paid the debt with my mind.

niggas fear what they don't, know
what they do, lie then believe
it, fear what they can't, shoulda
coulda wood teeth & nigger teeth
& juneteenth. niggas fear where
they come, a bullet for Janesha
cause she smile like mama, a
bullet for every door you hold
no key, i fear for the nigga in me,
the white in my head want him
dead, the nigga's scared he'll
come to work blastin, the nigga
in me dream, at risk of death by
waking, dream in a language
before the ocean, dream in
danger, dream exiled, dream
caged, dream back to the fields
& before the fields, fields, the
nigga in me dreams while the
white in me watches, scared of
dreams, & strapped.

we ate war, war had us, war it wasn't, we were. in a boat my mind went overboard, my mind freest amongst the sharks. they told me if i survived the ocean i could be a coin, bred to farm, farmed to breed & farm, a legacy of cotton i could sell you movie, book, or musical, *Slavery! Live!* the war of the boat, the belly of where i abandoned my mind to survive the body. i wasn't born, i was made & added to the tally. an animal owns nothing, all meat, even the brain, even the bite

music where my mind was, but even the blues went white, i don't know what my thoughts were away from them, admitting my mind makes me sick, my mind shacked up with their nonsense. free from white noise i'd probably just chill, feed birds after washing my hands of their throats. poetry happens, something to do with my hands that's not jail time, why lie tho, i'm a coward, a slave to slavery, it makes me a salary, i wanted freedom & they gave me a name, it's distracted me for long enough

they started building pillars at
the edge of my mind, they
were beautiful so i helped
them. my mind? in the field,
was a field, was fled too late.
years of lovely towers in the
distance, i ran to them but
couldn't leave, a tower to the
sky next to a tower to the sky
next to a tower to the sky
makes a cage. i was a prisoner of
my own design, helped patent
my chain, penned my pen,
& so on & so on & so *on*
i was with my mind turned off.

i had to break out my mind
to get it back, i needed to
see the words in the light,
with shadows, check their
color & fail them against
the paper bag. i needed to
peep my brain & the birds
on it, check who they
belonged to, who could eat
them, who they'd poison,
if they flew & who they'd
carry.

i had to move my mind outside my body

move my body like my mind

move my mind

deeper into the dark

question of its use

& that's when the poems got dangerous

& that's when their hopes became tangible

& that's what you should fear

& that's me laughing in the dark

with a star at my hip

& yes, it is what it looks like

i said the quiet part/   aloud/
i rehearsed my   action.

less hope

apologies. i was part of the joy

industrial complex: told them their bodies were

miracles & they ate it up, sold *someday*

made money off *soon* & *now*, snuck an ode into the elegy

forced the dead to smile & juke

implied America, said *destroy*, but offered nary step nor tool.

paid taxes knowing where the funds go.

in April, offerings to my mother's slow murder. by May

my sister filled with the bullets i bought. June & my father's life

locked in a box i built. my brother's end plotted as i spend.

idk why i told you it would be ok. not. won't. when they aren't

killing you, they're killing someone else. sometimes their hands

at the ends of your wrist. you (you & me) are agent & enemy.

there i was, writing anthems in a nation whose victory was my blood

made visible, mama too sugared to weep without melting, my rage

fed their comfort foaming from my racial mouth, singing

gospel for a god they beat me into loving.   Lord

your tomorrow holds no sway, your heaven too late.

i abandon you as you did me. c'est la vie.

but sweet Satan – OG-dark kicked out the sky

first fallen & niggered thing – what's good?

who owns it? where it come from?

Satan, first segregation, mother of exile

what you promise in your fire? for a real freedom

i offer over their souls. theirs. mines

is mines. i refuse any hell again. i've known

nearer devils. the audience & the mirror. they make you look weak.

they clapped at my eulogies. they said *encore, encore.*

we wanted to stop being killed & they thanked me for beauty

& pitifully, i loved them. i thanked them.

i took the awards & cashed the checks.

i did the one about the boy when requested, traded their names

for followers. in lieu of action, i wrote a book

edited my war cries down to prayers. oh, Devil.

they gave me God & gave me clout.

they took my poems & took my blades.

Satan, like you did for God, i sang.

i sang for my enemy, who was my God.

i gave it my best. i bowed & worse, smiled.

teach me to never bend again.

it doesn't feel like a time to write

being (Black) feels like a lot right now.
they shot a man then they shot

the people mourning the man.
they shot a man while he was

> a. handcuffed
> b. walking away
> c. already dead

the terrorists i fear played ball with the cops
or they is the cops. i ain't got much left to give

these poems, (Black) folks of every kind
of body are dying & yes at our own

hands too & before you start
pointing fingers wash yo blooddrunk

blooddrunk mind. if you still say
things like *we need all the info*

there must be a reason
then i can't waste

any more time on you.
i turn to the cards, the stars

G-d, the gods, my sweet dead, all them
say it's an age dead & walking.

the last of the whiskey, the portal of sex
bring me no peace.

i got a fear of being (Black) in public
& white folks were fed off to fear of me.

(nigg)agoraphobia has taken over the nation.
they killin' white babies now & still the paid-for prayers.

i've never been more afraid
of a white man's loneliness.

in my dreams all the (Black) folks
turn to ants & America is a toddler

stomping us out – she so damn excited
we can't get away. we die under her play all day.

                //

i'm just your average american: too broke &
late for brunch, looking
for a new job & hungover, just trying
to Netflix & fuck a little bit then you watch the news or
hear the worry in mama's voice when
she tell you be careful driving 'cause that ice
is slick & the law out there thick & she know both
can lead to *accident*.

                //

my friends are in the streets again because again
& again & so forth & how many more?

poems feel so small right now
my little machines fail me
all i've ever wanted to say:

        1. we are tired of your cancerous now

        2. until we are guilty & alive the same as you

        3. we beg for peace but you hear *fire, please!*

4. what you call country, we call plague

5. you say godgodgod but lobby his enemy's wishes

6. you are the soul's enemy

7. i free my we from your is and your will be

//

America, my burnt vanilla daddy
your lips turn into a cleaver
when you kiss my neck

//

if a white man who murdered is allowed
to be gentle & a Black girl murdered
is assumed at fault – when my baby get murdered –

                              there i go.
                              expecting.
                              pregnant
                              with knowing
                              your nothing future
                              & ache for bludgeoned yesterdays.

//

it doesn't feel like a time to write
when all my muses are begging
for their lives.

[this shadow haunting me again]

this shadow haunting me again

no good heffa curses the lights, monsters my arm

into birds, them dark ones, small murders found

between dusks, my black

field where the sins root best, still calling

them sins, the god i fled & savor

a mark on my language, pox of my soul

who turned my brain up this high?

the squirrel is a man & two breeds of beasts

before it's a squirrel, my shadow to crows

letters falling out songs, how cruel

sunlight is, those keys screaming *stay!*

October & the trees are on fire

dead fire under my feet when i walk

am i the ghost? it me who quiets at the bottom

of the sage? am i what came by window

seeking possession? own what? how time? i when? none

of my gold is real, green loops spook each finger

ears like moldy peas, the rot brown border

where each tooth meets the gum

proof? me expired? what if that was a stroke

in the car all those years ago?

what if i'm still there, shaking, dreaming?

shit dream, w/ rent & police & diarrhea

lackluster dick, three soulmates

& i scared them all off, too bland to be hell

too much blood to be an eternity

& the nausea in the morning

my weak stomach & weaker will

explain that? wouldn't something alive

see the pattern & redirect?

don't even the ants figure it out?

who killed me? stuffed me here?

lets my nothing hands drive that car? the neighbor's

prayers keep making holes in my floor

i've kept the most urgent ones out of spite.

her prayers panicked & stinking in their corner

i wait in mines on the angels.

(don't worry) if there's a hell below, we're all going to go –
chopped & screwed

amongst the trillions who singe who singe who singe
           who singe who singe who singe
    the trillions who singe who singe who sing
          who singe who singe who
the trillions who singe who singe who singe
      who singe who singe who singe
the trillions who singe who singe
       who singe
amongst the who singe but don't burn

or we are sectioned off into our loudest
sin or by the sum or do borders persist

do i get to see Franny again?
do i get to see Franny again?
down
down
down
down there, second earth, proof of the too high
not even our mothers made it. ain't pray

hard enough. if there's a hell we all end
up the devil's abundance. you not good:
i never been shit. casually wicked.
a citizen. that's how evil i be.
a zit of sin, that's how measle i be.
feel me? i voted. i agreed
i voted. i of greed.
i voted. i decreed.
          i agreed
to the kill. i'm full grown. taxes paid. i built the bomb.
i bloomed the cancer field under the hood.
i killed meemaw. i'll 'pologize when we
get down where she prayed the murder of me
  my gawd . . .

anti poetica

who cares how long i've spent with my poems – those shit psalms those rats of my soul –
headfirst thru the window me at their ankles demanding substance, revelation, sudden
gravity – shamed out my leafless, drug-shanked brain – this gray popper worn hell – that
dark dull circle i try to conquer beauty & the state from within. i'm not revolutionary
i'm regular. nothing radical in being America's enemy, the country of enemies. we find
our laughter between the horror. stop asking me to explain having a body & a mind & a
heart – their harmonies, their plots to murder each other. i've lived long in a low solstice –
wife to a pipe & the blue lit plain – leo trash – saved by occasional dick & the knowledge of
my mother, friends i confess my pocked seasons only after their close. arachnid moods –
self-cornered – text back weak – i haven't been much lately – the dark season lasted years,
swallowing seasons, collecting itself in my shallows like a motor-sheered fish. where did
the poems go? what is their trouble? what kinda water is i?

alive

danez, stop acting shook when Black folk
are alive, quit the dream of near
kill & early dirt, it's no dream.
free them boys caged in stone sonnets
you are not warden, not reaper, not
the fates, not their damned mama. alive
is a thing we can be too. look.

                        you are not dead & popeye's is
                        out of spicy. in heaven, they'd never.
                        in heaven, even they biscuits be moist.
                        but heaven ain't yours yet, them biscuits
                        dry as fuck, so God gave you
                        honey & tea & kisses & lovers
                        who spit in your mouth when asked.

the body is the body & inside
there's a person, imagine that? imagine Black
devoid of death, imagine us endless until.
if they kill you, they kill you.
until then they can't touch you, boo.
we all die, even God. don't run
from death, hide & let it seek.

                        four girls playing church with a stump
                        for a pulpit, reason enough for today.
                        you amen passing by, auntie trapped in
                        your deacon body. don't mean to look
                        like danger, but you were born boy'd.
                        but you don't smell like run, amen
                        gifted right back. heaven enough for now.

you can't take your quiet for granted.
five miles from peace there is mourning.
hunger walks by your window hourly. two
doors over, cruelty keeps its voice down.
you have to live despite despiteness, live
in the full context, not happy corners.
joy is not the antidote to suffering   it happens inside it. flowers & jokes
                                          at the funeral. i orgasmed at gunpoint.
                                          i know joy by its distance from
                                          terror. they're the same boy, his two
                                          hands meeting at a neck: a garland
                                          or a noose? they wore flower crowns
                                          at the wake. what magical, worthless royalty.

this what that grief do, leaves you
guilting your good days, weary of light.
i wish us a near, new world
where we die of cancer, crashes &
nobody hands, our hungers brief & gentle.
soon. we're alive there. who won't be?
let's sing while we plot their revenge.

"you don't even know me / i'm hanging from a tree"

you don't even know me, i'm hanging from a dream.

me? in my last life? savage. siren wet

& dreamlynched. me? was goodest pussy, nine lives all murdered

for my talent at my color, my sex, whatever he killed me for

i was the best at it. best blood-lipped dusk

best clotted sweetness, best bluing. me? once, i was born

the rope, not the neck. once, i was a fire full of niggers

(you know it's happened, someone's said that

someone heard about the building candled while full

of screaming lil wicks & laughed. i was never that laugh.)

i was the hymn of nearing sirens in the dying ear

announcing *not yet*, sound entering & touching the mind.

i was mine once

        & again in this life i'm mostly my own

somewhere far from your knowing, deep

in a Black mood, the wade of my heart making its way

to my brain carrying information, secrets, the rumor

of my body, the story i tell for wealth & the wealth

is worthless. they keep killing me, every time

i'm back by summer. i crawl out the sun. gold is useless

but in every life, i have it. look at me, up here

dangling like the poplar's hidden tongue, like my tongue.

look past the party at my feet, the children giddy

for a scorched finger. look me in what was my face

deep into the smoky pit i used to pray & kiss

find my final, plaque-worn star.

volta

this universe my most docile & stunted

weapons rounded into words, my work

so undangerous. they untapped my phone

found no threat, the shame i felt. my oppressors

fear me not. they see their chains

working. universe where i'm a match

head thrown back, laugh feeding the flame

as massa screams into kindling, teach me surprise

in the middle of obedience. give me the road

to that final glee, you giggling ash, shiver i feel

bowing my head on the street.

& universe where i'm a late queen, Christ-locked

& fat off Friday fish, rumor robed lonely

next to gray angels, i ask your late volta

long-avoided birth, that not-yet-then

-now, i need a new bravery. i don't want to live

a coward's peace. where's my mission?

what world comes if i use my hands?

headed

escape & *travel* mean the same to me. add *took*.
can't see *journey* & not see *flee*. *to run to*
implies *away*, *here* pointing at *left*.

little fugitive,
little used-to-slave,
   where does the map end?
little broke-out,
little dipped,
   where is freedom's home?
little off-the-chain,
little stole-back,
   there is a place where your blues is not fuel, coin
   unrequired & softer. i seen't it in a dream
   inside a hole in one's neck.

   a hole i put there.

Last Black American Poem

Voted for the negro twice, twice my captor
Wore my face. Admit it, Danez, you loved
Your master in your shade. Yes, I loved
Knowing the color at the end of my chain
Matched mine. ((Wrong river. It wasn't chains
It was water when one of us helmed the boat.
Water for our eyes, water raised to the lips
Of cargo. Still cargo. In summer
We turned down that Jeezy, learning a new one's
Slain name. The helm and still. The boat, still
Headed to Carolina shores.)) My president was Black
When mothers got millions in exchange for sons.
Michelle's perm was perfect as bombs dropped
In the middle of childhoods.
We buried my grandpa with an Obama button
Pinned to his lapel. Finally free, we sent him to heaven
American. When he won, we sprinted Bascom Hill
& danced like happy slaves at Lincoln's feet.
We were happy ass slaves, happy to vote
Happy to be able to protest the killing
We couldn't end, happy for healthcare
That killed us slower, happy the gays could marry
In the country where trans women vanished
Like snow in warm winters
Happy our wars were only of the mind
Only elsewhere.

Forgive me, I wrote odes to presidents.

1955

two hours west of Egypt, over in Money, that boy.
& his overripe face, river wrecked, no seed, no amulet.
my grandpa, sixteen & singing, still small, fear-steadied
years from his own violence, pulls the name from the radio
feathered & soaking, stunned blue by the current's silk trample
& keep. what a soft name, you must hum to begin him
mama's massacred lil man made maybe martyr, mural
haunting wallets, a warning tucked between nephews
his face. no face. that face. his. his name wounds time
his face a knife sinking thru centuries, but centuries don't fit
in a year or in a boy's guiltless hands, my grandpa, before
he was anyone's flinch, stood in the kitchen with crows
in his chest, he was no tree & yet in his hands a boy
dead enough to be an angel, too drenched to fly, my pa, a sky
stood in wait for the river to drain from wings.
where was your someone when the drowned refused flight
& Mamie left his mushy mug to wind & flies, flashes & eyes?
that year, Rosa utters a coordinated *no* & the world takes off
soon, my James takes a train north into another white cold kill
& that name still soggy & refused in his hands & all over
all he touches: his daughters, his wife's cheek, the split
hogs, where he is secret & plush, everything, wet with it.
listen – this is true – my grandma met him two summers
before then with his lil quartet, he bought her ice cream
& laid diddies at her flats. summer – that evil, bright constant –
changes a boy, fills him with awe, awe which can mean
terror. ain't never heard my James's song, not one lonely peep.

Approaching a Sestina on I-94 West

after Jane Huffman

escaping the known futures, your people rode into Minneapolis
thinking blood would spill less & do better up here, never saw
so few Black folks, but no stars & bars this far north.

sixty years later & you're not sure they shouldn't have kept south.
you fear the stars, on the other hand Ronda's cousin got killed at noon, law
didn't come until 4. you ran into the house crying to your mama grappling breasts

again, spooked since her mama died & the nurses didn't listen. her grief won't thaw.
it's been winter in her for eight years. she cook but don't eat, work so money happens, stress
her titties in the mirror all night. y'all moved, she barely noticed. at your new school over east

you read a poem about how niggas are trees. you think white folks must be the saw.
for homework, you wrote about Black mothers as crying trees living many apples less.
your teacher didn't get it, so you rewrote it as the apple dead not far from the tree. she loved it

now that she could see the dead body, asked you if you grew up over north
turned red when you say northeast, apologized too long, tries to relate, pressed
over whatever she pressed over, called you bright in a way you know she thinks your Black flaw.

when she asked if you like poetry, you said nah, lying, not wanting to talk to her anymore
not wanting to be here anymore, under the north star's lie, you could ride east
& live with your daddy but Chicago's no different, there too you knew nobody

who died, but you knew their mamas & brothers & friends & now you know one
you know teachers who don't know you, you know the video & what you saw
you know what the video & the dying does to a city, you know they killed your grandma

'cause nobody at Regions would listen when she said she was in pain, not even the African nurse
who your mama thought was cute could get the doctor to do shit. you wrote a poem
about how doctors are like cops to the body. the teacher didn't get it, the TA you like loved it.

she has braids you want & wordy tattoos. she smells like peaches & oil when she leans close.
she said she'll help you with your Spelman app so you can get the hell out of Minneapolis.
on the way from school, your tears froze. the last straw.

Dayton's Bluff

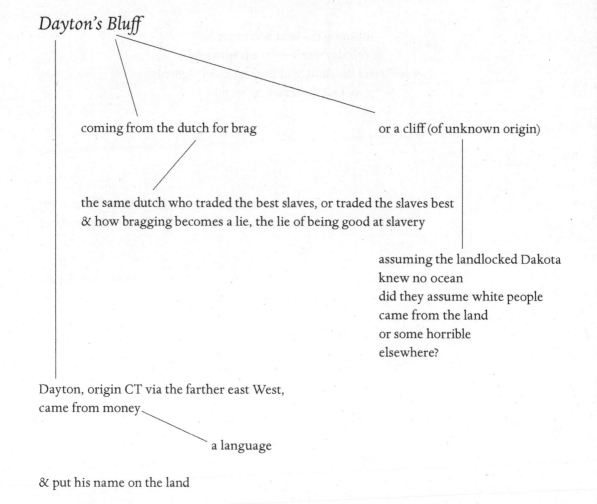

coming from the dutch for brag

or a cliff (of unknown origin)

the same dutch who traded the best slaves, or traded the slaves best
& how bragging becomes a lie, the lie of being good at slavery

assuming the landlocked Dakota
knew no ocean
did they assume white people
came from the land
or some horrible
elsewhere?

Dayton, origin CT via the farther east West,
came from money

a language

& put his name on the land

was it dayton's bluff

meaning his cock on the table was his name on the hill

or was it dayton's bluff

meaning a people had to be disappeared off the cliff for his legacy to rise

or was it dayton's bluff

meaning the land was never his
& one day won't wear his surname
& we'll end the theater of land acknowledgments
& end the lease/the leash?

whose disappearance will christen that nation?
who will first laugh humongous & free in the dead man's face?

i step onto the air
i know where we have won

rondo

If New York has its Lenox avenue, Chicago its State street, Philadelphia its Wylie avenue, Kansas City its Eighteenth Street, and Memphis its Beale street, just as surely has St. Paul a riot of warmth, and color, and feeling, and sound in Rondo street.

Earl Wilkins, *The St. Paul Echo*, September 18, 1926

By the 1930s Rondo was the heart of St. Paul's African American community, not only housing the majority of African American residents in the city, but also home to critical community businesses, organizations, and institutions. . . . However, by the late 1950s this tight-knit community would be shattered by the construction of Interstate 94, connecting the downtown business corridors of Minneapolis and St. Paul.

Initial expressway plan for the Minneapolis-St. Paul connection was known as the St. Anthony Route, which would [...] extend right through the heart of the Rondo neighborhood. St. Paul city engineer George Harrold opposed this plan—citing concerns about loss of land for local use and the dislocation of people and business—suggesting the alternative Northern Route, which would run adjacent to railroad tracks north of St. Anthony Avenue, leaving the street intact. Ultimately, the St. Anthony Route was chosen and approved by government officials citing its efficiency.

In 1955, Rondo community leaders Reverend Floyd Massey and Timothy Howard worked to lessen the effects of freeway construction and gain support for a new housing ordinance through the formation of the Rondo-St. Anthony Improvement Association. Their advocacy was successful in achieving a depressed (below-grade) construction of I-94, however, the route still split the Rondo neighborhood and forced the evacuation and relocation of hundreds of people and businesses. One in every eight African Americans in St. Paul lost a home to I-94. Many businesses never re-opened.

Although the neighborhood would never be the same, the spirit of Rondo lives on.

Gale Family Library

a south we built in dead Decembers, an Africa made of ice, a negro could work, daughters with sugar on theirs dreams, sons who didn't flinch at the potential of trees, dirt that couldn't grow the beans we liked, but a decent home & a good job, honkies that stared but didn't mob (as quick), winters we hated but could survive, just a few hundred miles south of what used to be freedom, we knew now so many years from chains & still so many in chains, that freedom wasn't something on this side of the boat, but at least a little more happiness, homes in our name, enough land to grow some collards & tomatoes, our Sunday daughters in white brighter than any snow.

many
we
negro
dreams
just
daughters
Africa
we

theirs
sons
home
survive
our
we
enough
freedom

Western Ave

a south made
of sugar[1]

an Africa
with

the potential of

honkies[2]
    we
  knew

Dale St

still

so many   chains
this side of

little

happiness[3]

land[4]

---

1. sweethomes they ruined with moneyrain, dissolved our new mississippis into neverheres
2. the promise of fear, their variable hunger for our various sufferings, neighbors who unwelcomed us
3. "freedom" was a door into a bigger cage & when they couldn't shackle the necks anymore, their metal met the mind, they chained time, chained the money, chained the dreams & noosed futures
4. yet we were Black and so forever, we sifted their violences for our gold & became their terrors for our safety

Dale St

sons dream dirt like[5]

winters mob
but we survive[6]

so many years from freedom[7]

quick, we grow our Sunday[8]

Victoria St

---

5. even the schools massacre their lil dreams, six feet tall or under, baby boys displaced into the city's carnivorous machine

6. yet they have not killed us

7. distant enough to see even they are not free, hate/greed/their god/their contempt all cages, slow funerals for the world they cellmate with us, locked in their disdain for tomorrows

8. in the church basement we praise, we plot, we fed & feed, we baptize, we redeem, we organize, we haul up, we sweat, we break down, we safe, we home & so here they come armed with torches, manifestos, badges, roads

Victoria St

like a virus we spread across the black paved over our new
Kenya, sick of ending under their leprous destiny, dying in
their dream that rots the future, we made them late for work,
traffic such a gentle revenge for how they clog heaven, a
small inconvenience in return for the harvesting of cousins

Lexington Pkwy

my Selby children! my
Fuller fam! my Edmund
kin! sisters of Jimmy
Lee! Minnehaha mamas!
my Laurel laureates!
my Hague homies! my
Ashland riders! boys
of the Victoria corners!
niggas outside Conoco &
uncles slanging swine on
University! my goddesses
leaving Shiloh Baptist &
Pilgrim! my Half-Pint
steppers! my Frogtown
dreamers leaping stars!
my minutemen! my
people & ya mama nem!
this land ain't ours, but
these blocks know us.
our blood, the river & the
blessing, our grannies the
haints

on the corners & in the
pines. no more us ending
us over things petty as
address, no more near
funerals we made with
our hands. let us protect
this, our fertile concrete,
green & stone bama, our
ever daughters. should
we make sacrifices, let
it be the pig with the
cannibal eyes, the bank
who murders with
money, the roads who
swallowed our history
whole. when i head on,
bury me in the median.
let my hollowed body be
a havoc bell until what
rings the air is no siren or
gunfire or griefsong, but
freer then freer then free.

METRO

after Jonah Mixon-Webster

Queen Performing "And I'm Telling You I'm Not Going" in a Blue Dress, Saloon Bar, Minneapolis, 07/2022

even tho i can see the safety pins
holding up the cerulean gown fastened into the dark
brown, glittery turtleneck we're supposed to believe
is starry skin, even if the wig is cheap
blond & begging your neck to stay still
should it fall & reveal the fuzzy cornrows
under your playsister's old stocking, even if the light
isn't dim enough to make that plastic
look like jewels or if the corset's outline
is a cracked bone beneath the blue
stretch fabric neon & unforgiving,
the lipstick a shade too light & the rouge
a touch too much   the song
is running thru you like a July
black sky's electric kink
                              i'm here
weeping at your feet, three dollars
held out like a first prayer or the last
prayer before the rest of your life.

who has seen me – barely held together –
not worth a dime or a damn – night
stained under eyes – bloodbroken – begging
a coffin nearer & soonish – my blues
the only thing to my name – my name
walking out on me?
                    no will. no way.
        & i am. i still *am*. i was
so close to the close of my era, my period
thank God, turned into commas, enough
to make the rent, the lights, to eat, to hand
a woman, raggedy & divine, what i can spare to lose.
released, spared of my own midnight plots

the long, blurred years i slugged
after my blood turned to shit, leaking flies when i cried.
now, the same blood that seeks to end me – that i sought
to end – keeps me alive. what? my blues keep me
warm, not blue-lipped, not cold & unmourned.
                              how?
i'm not gonna leave you, i'm telling you
tomorrow is what the stars told me
waits at their edge. the sun is just
a brighter night. we survive more
than we know. my fragile & fabulous fam
– you Black, latecome daughters –
– you Black, duskfound sons –
– you Black, bluesborn somebodies –
hooked here by blessings too small to call miracles
we can outlive our nightmares into our dreams, girl!
you, like me, who blueprinted your own finales
you, like me, who script your murders on your enemy's behalf
i'm telling you –
i'm staying –   i'm staying –
        – & you – & you – & you

Dede was the last person i came out to

after Angel Nafis

why did i long to leave the man i wasn't
uncomplicated beneath your blade?

in that brief, weekly mecca, i wanted nothing
to mark me but the edge of your sheer

cutting horizon above my brow. our romance
of money & mirrors, we trade coins

for beauty & peace. in the time-rich forever
of this shedding place, the million doors

to this heaven we attend to be tapered & grown
i didn't want my facts to become the news

nor the closeness it takes for a man to square a man
into grace to be soured by desire or gods

or traditions that leave my kind unloved, unhoused
unknown by clippers, raggedy & unbrothered.

Dede, i wasn't a man. i was your clay
afraid of being banished from your hands.

loose me not from this uncled oasis
where i rather be misnamed than uncounted.

i curved the men i kissed into vague women
in that chair, stretched my life so thin

you could cut it with a whisper. i knew the world
had sharpened & accrued its jagged disciplines

i knew the world & needed this one place in it
not to be it. but then, you found my poems. & then

you cut my hair.

Jesus be a durag

after Jamila Woods

& be mighty, black satin savior stretched around my scalp
take me in your hand & make me like the water. be a way
to tell my people i am their people, sheer cape falling down

my neck make me superhero, captain save a hoe
from myself, rag to make my unragged mornings
let me wake up Black & alive & Black & alive & thinking i'm cute.

lord of lawds, be a fence around my fly, be shield, be rock
be spell, be a dark & lovely magic, sweet Jesus, if you God
be God, let whatever reaches toward us to end us slick pass.

let America drown in our waves, if a bullet must touch us
let it graze soft as a bristle brush, let us spill no blood on a day
we feel beautiful & we be beautiful, let us know it, be casket

sharp & banned from early caskets. no Black person will die in this poem
but these waves might hurt somebody, watch yourself, swim good
be happy we sleep with these rags on. i heard a story once about

a boy who brushed his hair for forty days & forty nights & when he
finally slept he forgot to wrap his ocean up. same night, mamas
started crawling from his hairline carrying babies, men climbed

out his waves like they had just jumped off the boat, a wet army
necromanced from naps. see? this hair is a right kind of holy. see?
it's not hair at all. on top of our dome, a prayer carrying us home.

I-35W North // Downtown Exits

Minneapolis, my murderer, my mother
ship, my moose heart, my mercy
will end in you. nearing your southern face
you almost look safe, so beautiful
you could stare too long & miss the ice
winter the most innocent killer here.
i remember you purple blazed when Prince passed
the sky plum-stained, bridges bruised violet
so gorgeous, you liar. you didn't miss him.
you wanted money for his missing.
Minneapolis, my liar, my murdered mother,
my mercy road-killed, my ship-belly burial
in a frozen lake, your promise is death
done nicely, a smile a sorry with your bullets
you kneel never at altars
your kneeling prays the fathers away
dresses streets in flame.
you're the only thing to burn
& come out whiter.
where the people raged, you build a business.
i don't trust your purple lights
(blue on red on blue on red)
i don't trust your purple
(the cops could be anywhere).

Minneapolis, Saint Paul

It happened again. This time, they did it with a knee. Cause of death: twenty bucks, police. For George Floyd, the crowd stretches down Chicago Ave, cutting the city through the Third Precinct, just how I-94 once ripped Rondo without question or apology. On Hiawatha, a few blocks from the now-destroyed precinct, there's a day-care playground full of little Black kids. Sun-blessed, little fades and puffs and hijabs, little hands gripping the fence, little feet jumping, jumping, little mouths a chaos of smile and chant. "Black Lives Matter! Black Lives Matter!" They say it with their teeth and whole bodies. When was the first time that they knew those lives mattered? Do these toddlers already know that some propose counterarguments? When we make it to the precinct, my love and I join the line flanking westbound Lake Street, and for us the protest is one of guarding others. We wade through the rain redirecting cars, only two or three of them giving us grief. As the rain picks up and the crowds disperse, we start the three-mile walk back to the car and we see the precinct up close for the first time since arriving. A busted door, folks at the windows and on the cars. Good, I think to myself. Though I'm scared. Cops love cops and buildings more than they love the people. Five blocks from the precinct and the sounds rush our ears. The boom-boom-boom-boom of flash grenades, tear gas, the drum of rubber bullets hitting protesters, the sounds of something, everything, dropping.

:::

The Target is on fire. Frankly, I couldn't give less a damn. I love me some Target, but Target doesn't have a body. Tonight, Black Twitter is cracking up at the video of a white woman trying to defend Target with a seemingly sharp object. An army of one Karen against a revolt, and she's there to protect what exactly? She gets a few knocks to the head and a fire extinguisher's cloudy laugh to the face. Already, the people out of whom capitalism would make an unmemorable meal are flocking to defend the brands. These people find their rage in the disruption of their comfort. "Won't someone please think of the Arby's?" seems like a very weird place to put your concern. What America are you mourning? Target wasn't in the fields, cotton-bloodied hands. Walmart never hung from a tree.

:::

it wasn't poetry when
polyester-blend knee anviled
the lover's gulf & bet

                                    we were in the streets
                                   next day no question
                                  was proposed by knee
                                 the weight was an answer
                                  i was there wherever
                           i go when we are murdered
                              my usual shoes usual rage
                              new name same who when
                           i looked up there was smoke
                           but there was smoke before
                               i could smell it now good
                              stink of a burning finally
                              ours not the blaze of guns
                                or the devil's tax or his
                                hot stone plantations
                        no, like *fire* fire like the wind
                                      cradling the brick
                                    i didn't know brick
                                could burn i didn't know
                              Wendy's was so flammable
                     i loved every minute of it i pissed
                             my skivvies scared i prayed
                     for this then God showed up with it

                                         i wasn't ready

                                       :::

When I go to Midway to clean up with my mama and my broom, I'm sad to see the Foot Locker is gone, but only for the memories of matching tall tees with the homies, the parties we dressed ourselves for, only to be stopped by cops for wearing the same color. Foot Locker will be fine. I'm pissed at whoever busted the windows out of Best Steakhouse, but I forgive them. I'm worried about who is going to get to rebuild the now-burnt and burning Twin Cities, if neighborhoods in St. Paul and Minneapolis will be further gentrified by flame. Capitalism is the worst bird, able to make a tool out of its destruction. Bad phoenix. How do you kill the unkillable thing? The thing that builds the most dangerous and violent houses: the precincts, the banks, the courts, the boardrooms, the leasing office, the capitol.

:::

what misnamed hunger. not
a hunger, but a right. something to do
with need. someplace to take
a bit of what's due, those notorious
been owed acres come up
someone else's gold. run it.
gimme the loot.
a robin steals gold wire
for her nest. for a week, rain
thieves the light late May.
this way. glass like water
breaks. the fire was no mother
it was our furious sister. who cares who
first birthed this son-waned moment.
mama, take what you need.
shoes, purses, tvs, food, even
if it was just the sound
of one thing breaking outside
your soul, snatch it
how they pluck us from summer.
fuck them people
who made a property of us
daughters handed down
with the estate.
a boat, a jail, a tax.
a law, a tree, a force-fed god.
all the ways, us taken from us.
for too long our rage been sleep
inside our grief.
rob them deep.
if no peace, get you a piece.
you could never gather
in the life of your arms
the sum of what was
stolen & stolen.

:::

My love and I leave a pretty tame protest to go get pizza right quick; we've been forgetting to eat these past few days. Most folks in the city are probably short on sleep, ignoring the demands of the body. Heading back downtown, the energy has changed since we left. What happened? The cops showed up, anger-drunk and tear gas in hand. Folks peacefully marching in the street has turned into rubber bullets to the body, and crowds scattered in fear. We loop downtown on foot, from corner to corner, until we end up on a street trapped by MPD in riot gear in our faces, the sheriff's department to our backs. When was Covid? What infection did I fear last week? The cops are the sickness.

:::

I've been raised to be wary. I've always been scared of the cops—the fear was passed like a name. Not scared, or not showing it, are the Black women on the other side of the police from me. Their voices are shred to ribbons of yell. Who fights for Black people more than Black women? Warrior matriarchs of our fed-up kingdom. Ribbons of chant, ribbons of *no justice* and *fuck you*. I'm a little braver next to them. I follow. Rattled and eyes stung, we make it home. Who is checking in on Black women? Who is fighting for them, their peace? In Kentucky, Breonna Taylor's murderers walk free, cops who shot up an EMT's home in the middle of a pandemic. Who else have we lost to cops, lost to white folks who deputized themselves, forgotten among the never-ending repetition Justice for Justice for Justice for Justice for Justice for . . .

:::

wasn't no stanza in the new river
of broken pipe & building resin
no stanza under the bridge
after curfew no rhyme launching tear gas
like careers no couplet blooming
between the nape & the knee no
matter how many times you run
it back no ode calling for their gone
mother soon reunited no metaphors
in the tanks downtown no sonnet
boarding up the tender glass
no poem tagged evidence in the morgue

:::

The beauty of the food drive makes me cry, the piles of bread and diapers rushed from cabinets and retrieved from the burbs. The beauty of the cleanup makes me cry, the brooms sweeping glass into a bag that a stranger steadies. The people cleaning graffiti off bank windows makes me laugh. The old Sheraton turned into a community-run shelter makes me cry, the blessing of owning a key to something. My grandma's spaghetti makes me cry, 'cause I couldn't have imagined stirring sauce and boiling water that day. The semi driver who, in my eyes, tried to murder people peacefully gathered on the bridge makes me cry, especially when the governor says that he was just "frustrated," like that's an excuse, like many haven't died along the short road of a white man's temper. The National Guard on my street makes me cry—it's barely noon and here are their armored vehicles and guns, no other reason than to announce themselves. The tears like fire down my face.

:::

Someone's starting fires on Northside. Northside, far from the protest, far from the noise and flame of the exhausted many. Northside, where the Black people are. Someone's setting fire to the Black. My apartment is a blink's distance from where the National Guard has set up, on the border between the south and downtown. We've smelled smoke for days, put out a few fires too. Who is protecting us besides us? What are these cops protecting?

:::

> we formed neighborhood watches
> after word spread of white boys
> lighting fires in dumpsters
> same time as blue boys
> downtown bashing Black heads
> of women screaming toward justice.
> we patrolled midnight from our curfew
> on rooves, balcony & month-to-month lawn
> until we became suspicious of anything
> unpoliced in the dark & became
> the pigs ourselves, our brothers
> downtown continuing to cloud
> tomorrow's mothers with tear gas.

an evil but brilliant strategy. light a few
fires & everyone become a match.

my neighbors are dying.
my neighbors are killing.
my neighbors are hungry.
my neighbors are suspicious.
my neighbors are Black.
my neighbors hate Blackness.
my neighbors are owed.
my neighbors owned my neighbors.
my neighbors are stolen.
my neighbors are landlords.
my neighbors were robbed.
my neighbors in the ground.
my neighbors are starved.
my neighbors profit.
my neighbors weep.
my neighbors drink.
my neighbors are in need.
my neighbors want for nothing.
my neighbors are fugitives.
my neighbors are hunters.
my neighbors are dying.
my neighbors assist.
my neighbors are aiming
at my neighbor's head.
my neighbor's hands on the phone ready
to summon my neighbor's blue death.

:::

Early, we ride out, strapped, to see the damage, the smolder where some bit of city used
to be. Rolling downtown to see what it's like, we find the police. Guns ready, armored
vehicles posed, flanking the whole way down Nicollet Mall—the Brooks Brothers, the
boutiques, the Target all protected, served.

:::

Still the children and mothers and uncles in cages at the border. Still the prisons packed like a boat's stinking hold filled with whom we come from. Still the drones circling above a farther sky and dropping our taxes made explosive. Still the forty-fifth president of death does the evil of presidents with less style to make it look like good. Still the police say to shoot us on the scanner. Still they plow into us by car and bullet and choke hold. Still the Taser and the gun "mistaken" for a Taser. Still they say "vote," like ballots are shields. Still the white supremacists running around the city, in and out of uniform. Still I have some hope. The school board abolished the police from the halls (and later did not). The Neighborhood Watches sprung up across the city and make the night a more secure world (until we became our own cops). If you are reading this and you've never been scared of the police (or yourself), I envy that silly dream, the dream where money guards your door with guns. Why do we have police? Have you ever googled where they come from? The precinct's ancestor is the plantation cabin filled with overseers, between the slave quarters and the big house. When the North came down to free my people, you tell me what burned?

:::

if the cops kill me
don't grab your pen
before you find
your matches.

:::

June came. With it, the heat. Every window, every wall, every random pipe and mailbox and concrete, flat stretch bloomed into canvas, into billboard, into propaganda, into plea. On some blocks *unity* reads like *we got this*, on others it sounds like *calm down*. Some wood burst with color and Black faces, some simply with the nearest spray paint say *Black Owned, Minority Owned, Kids Live Here*. Murals and graffiti jewel the city as it thinks about what it would mean to shed the things that hunt our skin. The officers are arrested and then out on bail, change still slower than fire. Elsewhere, Breonna's killers still sleep sound as she should have. Elsewhere, companies and institutions drop statements and videos and reading lists and graphics and specials. NASCAR banned a flag but couldn't find a noose. Another Black man dead. Another Black, another Black Trans, another Black Trans woman murdered and another. Round the corner from me, the brewery up the street put up a 8"x11" printer paper picture of George Floyd up in their half-block of floor-to-ceiling windows I've never seen one of us inside. I hate it here. It's June so it's perfect. They do it every Pride Month, take Stonewall and hide the brick. They're doing it again. Money making uprising a strategy, a mask. Money making your dead face a shield, an invitation to spend your grief. Money figuring out how to stay safe. Money playing the money game. Money making you forget it's about money. This all started over twenty bucks.

relativity

it's been centuries inside this grief
& since, electricity in the home
then in the hands, but – still – the fields
then the gravity under a collapsed sun
& each bullet its own star
& the gravity under that knee, that hold
that seemed to send time echoing
back & forward & still. like sound
from a bell, bleeding from the sky
& still stuck inside dancing until dead.
love the bell, cruelty the ringing
grief the ear that catches the sound
we the air, disrupted, cruelty's song
moving through, we survive –
or don't – the notes. it's not just
the field, or what burrows through
space to sweep us from earth
everything its weight
everything its pull, its horizon
morphing our brief event. & love
too can lock us out of time
& may you knew or know
or collide into that tether & stall.
but know today, which by this time
was ages ago, it's gonna take
too many tomorrows to get through
yesterday, i pray for time
to deal with now. no, i pray *to* Time.

anti poetica

hate the poem when you read it.
your thoughts on the poem
like an unwarranted & judgy nipple.
the problem with being
a poet is once others know.
the problem with poetry is humans
write it, not birds. the birds
are fascists, the fish say.
always someone shows up to detail
the murderer's kindness. i could
kill someone, i think i could
live with that.
i use the poem to trick my eulogist.
they'll speak of my heart, they'll allude
to wings, no mention of the ink
on my hands that smelled of iron
or the man missing from his life.

principles

i.

ask not what your country can do for you
ask if your country is your country (it's not)
ask if your country belongs to your country folk (the rich)
ask if your country is addicted to blood (it eats)
ask if your country is addicted to forgetting (it knows)
ask if your country is an oilhead or murderfiend (it craves)
ask if your country shakes at night starving
for bodies if bodies mean your country (your warden)
keeps on being your country in the same ol' ways (it do)
ask if your country was built off robbed land
& stolen breath (it was), if democracy (your lie) is a leash
tight as new skin around your neck (it chokes)
ask if your comfort means elsewhere
someone is burying a daughter (she blues)
ask if your comfort means round
the corner a man is dead 'cause a cop
mistook his fear (his education) for a gun (empty hands)
ask if your comfort (your bargain) means broke schools
& food deserts on the other side of town (your agreement)
ask if your new apartment used to belong
to someone who couldn't afford to look (the mirror)
like you, ask yourself if all the things
unpolite around the dinner table
are the dirt filling
a boy's hungry throat.

ii.

all lives don't matter
the same as all lives

some lives matter
only to themselves

some lives matter
only they hood

some lives matter
of fact & some lives
up for debate

all lives matter
to someone

what our life
matter to you?

      iii.

Diamond Reynolds is a hero
where no one should have to be a hero
(are we heroes for surviving? for being terrorized?)
steady as she can be with daughter
in the back seat & Philando (who fed children
who will not be protected from what
was legal in his hands)
slowly becoming a memory
right next to her, gun still pointed
at his body, cop outside the window
scared of a man he already
turned into a myth. thinks him
zombie when he already
imagined him ghost.
Diamond be diamond strong
in a world who treats our people
like bad water. Diamond
unbreakable but why they
test her like that? why they
send bullets through us
like they trying to see if we real

or just a bad dream? why they
american dream us into beast?
why they comfort the cops
& not the families?
why administrative leave?
why they look up the record
before they check the pulse?
why they try to spin the story
before they call the ambulance?
why they more worried about
getting caught than they worried
about the killing? why they
protect & serve themselves
from us? why they want us to
apologize for housing the bullets?
what good is police?
why hasn't goodness saved us?
how has goodness maimed us?
how long have i been so polite
accommodating my murders?

iv.

i don't want America no more.
i want to be a citizen of something new.
i want a country for the immigrant hero.
i want a country where joy is indigenous
as the people.
i want a country that keeps its word.
i want to not be scared to drink the water.
i want a country that don't bomb other countries.
i want a country that don't treat its people
like a virus. i want a country not trying
to cure itself of me. i want a country
that treats my mama right. i want a land
where my sister can be free. i want a country

that don't look at me & my man & think
about where & how we should burn.
i want a nation under a kinder god.
i want justice the verb not justice the dream.
i want what was promised to me.
i want forty acres & a vote that matters.
i want no prisons & a mule.
i want all lives to matter.
i want to be over with race
but race ain't over me.
i want peace. i want equity. i want guns
to be melted into a mosque, a church
someplace for us to pray toward better gods
& i wanna stop praying for my country
to be mine, for it to put the gun down
take the bomb back.

(*i don't want a country*
look at what countries have done
the borders perform a killing floor
i don't want a country
look at what countries do
please kill the state
within me)

v.

hope is hard
but i have it
i look at my students' hands
& imagine all that they will mother.

Christ, name i was raised to pray to.
Allah, sweet lord of my father.
all you gods of my homies & gods of strangers

gods within & ungodded tomorrows, work together
to build us into tools to build
a world we are grateful for
not grateful in spite of.

let us not be idle or stunned by fear
not be so comfortable that we ignore
another's grieving instead
of ending what forces her grief.

let us not be scared of the work
because it's hard
let us move the mountain
because the mountain must move.

let us, lords above us & within
be useful to our neighbors
& tender their wounds
be more bandage than blade
unless the blade is needed.

let us be a plague against what does not
bring us closer to home

be deadly to whatever fails us

& to whom.

poem

> I was born a Black woman
> and now
> I am become a Palestinian
> against the relentless laughter of evil
> there is less and less living room
> and where are my loved ones?
>
> *June Jordan, "Moving towards Home"*

he calls them "the children of darkness" & being one myself –
having been plucked from between stars, having been born again
in the dark, dark bellies of those ships, delivered as cargo
into the suffocating light of America – i find my kin.

"human animals," he called them & having been ape, been dog
been mongrel, cattled & culled, i knew who was my brother.

this late in empire, late meaning near its end not near its completion
let my language be clear & dangerous as water.
let my mind's tongue move sound, be exact
with where venom is intended & where light sought.

animals. he called them animals.

Free Palestine

said the birds

Free Palestine

said the fish

Free Palestine

said the mice

Free Palestine

said the mountain lions

Free Palestine

said the cattle

Free Palestine

said the wolves

Free Palestine

said the horses

Free Palestine

said the bats

Free Palestine

said the elephants

Free Palestine

said the deer

Free Palestine

said the squirrels

Free Palestine

said the bears

Free Palestine

said the wildebeests

Free Palestine

    said the geckos

Free Palestine

    said the snakes

Free Palestine

    said the dogs & cats

Free Palestine

    said the bees

Free Palestine

    said the spiders

Free Palestine

    said the ants

Free Palestine

    said the rhinoceroses

Free Palestine

    the birds again

nature

i hear your prayer.
i see your terror.
i know my teeth.

big head

i seen't too much. i read the ink
between the stars. i heard God's
voice, it left me swollen this way.
why couldn't i just die under
that gravity? now
i think in three-part harmony
i wonder the house down to bits
i see birds & know too much
about the mice they left motherless.
eyes so wide i see between time
i gaze the mirror & know its past.
why didn't you burst me, lord?
they call me watermelon head
no idea i can hear the seeds
screaming toward green in the dirt
or hear next week's rain
gathering around dust in the clouds.
you see red petals, i can see the light
gnashed & hemorrhaging inside
the hungry rose. don't tell me
to smile, i know what God
sounds like, i heard God's language
&, cursed, kept living. i'm thinking
everyone's thoughts. the acute
& rigorous evils we plan
for one another. the son
the father, i think them both.
we want to kill us. now
my neck aches from all this
knowing, my head threatens
to steal the moon. if i fell
face flat, earth would shiver
into doom. i could
headbutt the mountain
into glitter. a bullet to the skull

couldn't tickle my dreams.
in my left ear, squirrels
waiting out winter, whispering
about their savior. in my right
a mother bird is plucking
the weakest from the nest
they land at my feet
like prayers refused.
my tears dry by the cheek
my blink last all week
& i got a woman
hanging on each lash.
if you love them
unnoose them from my stare
then free me from this air.

i'm not bold, i'm fucking traumatized

same niggas i write poems for call me *faggot* & my utopia shrinks.

      who really do i mean by *we*?

    //

when you say *bravery* i think   what else?
don't we all brave a thing? even just the dark? through it

or deeper, darker still. i talk so loud
'cause i'm trying to find the door.

    //

i'm not every nigga!

      they not all in me!

i'm not that damn large! i contain multitudes
of little shit that only adds up to basic me!
    i only know a tiny percentage of all the Black people!
when i say *Black people* i mean what i've confirmed
in small circles of the niggas i know!

by *niggas* i know i mean niggas i choose! & i choose them all. i really do
mean to. but surely there's a list of niggas i rather not
        allow into my heaven
          absolutely a list of Black folks i pray toward hell.

    //

like, do Black presidents get to go to heaven?
or people who beat their children

to relieve stress? is the nigga who raped me gonna
be in thug mansion too? how heavy is my stone on his scale?

how much & what kinds of violence are allowed
within God's love? i know love

is some shit i'll never get 'cause my grandma
hopes my grandpa is waiting in her heaven

wings closed into a fist on his back.

     //

i have like four white friends, maybe
a dozen if i'm being generous & that feels brave

enough. you know what i'm talking about, all the little deaths
in their loving you, all of them. read *Citizen*

if you need that lesson. every teacher
those three semesters i got to know a deeper sad

added *Citizen* to the syllabus late, every one
of their white hands handing me what

i had already read & knew & they were
so amazed & with Trump the opportunity

for us to "finally write political poems" & it was
like they were just now opening their eyes

& all us once shadows had shapes, proper names.

     //

does it bother you when somebody talks
about your people, as a concept, right

in front of your face? what does your skin feel
like when it's evaporating into theory? mine, like sugar
dissolving in the sleeping mouth, taking the tooth with it.

//

the problem with being a poet is the line
so thin it's not a line where your history (personal)
becomes your history (collective). some folks
in my family can't get that to tell my story
i have to confess theirs. we are not stains
in the lives of others, not wind nor flat actors
nor tricks of light. we have shapes & make noise
& make scars & disturb & interrupt
& salve & slave & slip so easy from background
character to God
                    maybe we do start as wind.

//

my people ain't even my people. their utopia
calls for my death & they dress for the occasion.

it's some bullshit. it's impossible. i feel bad for poems
all we expect them to hold. the people

in my poems don't agree with my ways.
my poems shrink. i look to form

when my heart feels placed
in a blender & left to wait to pulse

that's what it feel like, feel like
when i remember who want me gone

& how i love them alive.

The Slap

there's no love there, so the words won't come
or it's not my love so i can't speak on it

& my hands knew before my brain
which sent me here to capture

some faulty papers flung into electric space
about the hand meeting the face

& how somehow this sets Black folks back
into the fields & up the trees. i want Black people

free from my decisions. i want my actions to be mine
& useful. i wish my cruelty to wither

& hopefully my karma has come. fuck the things
i've said about Black women in public

things that were overheard or deleted
things i meant to harm & things i said because

i'd been taught to say them. i am a faulty ally.
i've thrown hands to defend, yes

but i've also fired those bulleted words. i knew
which insults would hit & said them.

someone has the receipts, the scar.
i called Tanya, so beautiful and so kind Tanya

who was good to me & who i loved, "dark"
in a way meant to hurt & it did.

her disappointment haunted me for years
i was so small when i said it; so grown

by the time it left my dreams. there was my proof
i too could hurt the people i love.

what good was me wailing on my grandfather's face
to allow her off the floor

if i had already begun to turn his evils
into traditions? at the end of my action

was a Black girl crying. someone should have knocked
me out. i wish i was better earlier.

i wish a world where Black women are safe.
sweet wish, i am starward now, this is my goodbye.

my apology will be distance (but distance
would mean a life with no Black

women, which is a life to no heart or heaven.
i'm guilty? yes. but guilt is what i feel? no.

it's grief that whelms me. what light did i kill
in a Black girl? what soft, original part of me

had to die for me to hurt her? what brutal fraternity
did i invite in to pilot my hands & tongue?

what dies when a Black girl cries?
& what gains an arm?) no, not distance.

keep me here & let me fumble into life
as a steward of your peace.

my prayer: may the world be a Black girl's cake.
my promise: or burn it down.

ars america

my country wants to kill my daddy.

my country. my daddy lives

like he wants my mama dead.

my mama. The Father is silent

when daddy drunk & double fisted.

no God. mother nature kneels

in my mother's garden, readies their flowers.

The Joke

pretty much my first career: to take
Friday's horror & make it Wednesday's humor.
the swelling had ended & so the laughter could bloat
on the porch, only kin of bloodlock & marriage bed
James, you just drunk
just like her, akimbo & decades tired in her tone
just drunk! i don't understand!
   do grandma again, nezzy!
just drunk!
what made me weep & hide & fist-in-his-back weekends
now was my currency of cute, a requested delight
go to hell, Barbara! just go to hell!
   & how papa be lookin, neno?
stumble & cuss king, batter god, weekend dragon
punished if not friendly & in love with him on Monday
after the sabbath's purple-eyed theatrics
   wait! wait! wait! what grandma say again?
& again it goes: the joke, the laugh, the good days' end
the weekend, the liquor, the cuss, the blood or not,
the fist or not or fist, the saving or not or rescue & stay
the lines perfected & hook on time
& the cheeks well-rehearsed in impact & smile
his own mama beat bloody & quiet down on that farm
he hated his father as he studied him
i hated him from the stop of the stairs
memorized both parts, preparing myself
to love like a husband, take it like a wife.
not complicit, i was charged
to make it gold, sugar it.
i was the smallest, it was my precious duty
to turn the lip's blood & dusky eye's puss
into tears soft as giggles on our faces.

i miss that negro

tho i don't know if he'd love me or what
i'd lie about to be loved, but i like to think
we'd be cool & sometimes i'd call him after i knew

he was up & ask "what the hell you doing, old man?" & he'd say
"shit, boy, sleep" & we'd holler over all the mannish
nothings he'd been told to hush up bout

round a smaller me & what cancer looted, we'd have:
a few Stroh's & new grudges, his hard learning
of the fag he prophesized & believed cured, or maybe

he knew before he went unknowable, maybe if the
prostate had shrunk instead of molded he'd have got right
even a decade or two of not beating his wife

or maybe he would've again & you know what? we'd love him.
you can knock your father cross the jaw, test the barrel
to his neck & be bubble-gut giddy bout the dude

in the same weekend. i've tested the theory, i know
its empty, warm logic. i hated my beloved. the woman
he beat for forty years won't let you call him shit but a good man.

she is of a god that confuses & nourishes & imprisons me
he is in a good man's hell serving a good man's sentence
hate that marriage means to plot your escape & love's murder.

hate he taught me that. our local & occasional evil.
our shelter & from where we fled. a father. a country. i plotted
his death in dark of Saturdays. i'd kill the world to kiss him.

love poem outside of

understanding / would begin
in selfishness & end
in worse commitments. to live near
violence is not to own it
nor to be owned
but to belong to it
as the day
belongs to the sun.
dawn is a condition of
the way you are a condition of
if gravity is what sets the agreement
that pulls the earth's face round into light
then like dawn, whatever stayed me
pulled the hand nearer into
its daily events

    i stayed because
    i stayed because

i had a key & so kept returning myself
to my cage, cleaning it, adding girls
& teaching them to love you

    i stayed because
    i stayed because

when his hands rushed to me like comets
anything could happen

    i stayed because

knew no women who ever left
did not want to be the first woman

i stayed because

reason has no weight

when i buried him

    i cried because
    i cried because

Colorado Springs

she crying for all us – her brother, son, me, everyone someone's boy – before

the wedding, henny-wrecked, lovewhelmed, meaning well   *so much* –

she says – *Black boys go thru these days: gay, transgender, gangbanging* – i know

what she means, i try to   not be criminalized   i know she doesn't see us as crimes

maybe sins, but sense to her, since i know my own mother – i know she means

the bodies we didn't think our sons would lay down, the men we never imagined

would seek our sons in the night   our boys   dressed in those colors

monochrome & prism-strained, flagging what we hoped wouldn't find them. i know

when i pressed my purple stone to my mother's breast, what flooded her wasn't disgust

but sickness, knowing what violences might rush her once blue babe now cut to pink

meat, red as honesty, those blood-ill premonitions: love – their own bodies – other boys

all mothers know anything can hunt a son – a fear so animal language cannot tame

nor reason. later, before the wedding, in the woods at the mountain's feet, love

points out a mushroom *that looks like a coin*. it do. earthy currency, a metal soft

& chewable, fragile platinum. even if i was Mother Earth i couldn't expect this

wild change, fleshy & star-bright steel bloom. i wouldn't know it grew like this

too, dirt rising into armor. she didn't know we grow up fine, my mother loves

her purpled child deeper & truer even though what she feared would scar me

left its mark. i know she meant well, i know love shoots beyond language or sense.

mothers, if we make it, we make it through it all.

love, find our sons.

body, hold our babies well. free them from all cages even if it's what we named them.

violence, don't lust after our boys & call it kin. if you must find our babies in the midst

of their lives, leave a wound we can dress.

& may we not be the scars they stitch lonely in the mothergone dark.

Denver

the go-go dancers must be angels
humming the shadows
even bassless
the dark flutters around them
their bodies like stone
thrown into the lake of time.
the weed is good
this high up, it's still not heaven
but we spend the day in clouds
playing *could we live here?*
surveying the bar
forecasting memories, poppers
between could-bes & ifs
& i know, even though
it's still America
it's not mine
i don't know this place's sins
ignorant as a man new to heaven
ready to rest, expecting his mother
instead issued a robe
& put in his place
before instructed to sing forever.
i forgot where i was.
the angels in prison.
with you, i'm almost free.
the weed is great.
every land has & will hunt its elegies.
i've seen too much to see heaven.
i could write mine anywhere.
with you, i'm free to not have a mind.
we could move anywhere
& the world would find us.
i could die anywhere.
i tie my life to you.
bring the dark.
i hear humming.
angels. angels. angels.

Sioux Falls

where the water crashes into the quartzite, i love you
though our joints cuss us for leaping the islands
of stone striped by meek rivers, though there is more
us to touch than when we first met as hungry strangers
naked but for the socks & my pink jock, i love all that new you
folding round as we cross where the ducks are sick of us
though you hate it, i lay my head there, when i am sick of sound
i rest my ear where you breathe & rumble, i love that gut
that i love every day which you don't notice until we make way
across the water where the water above meets the water below
& their touch makes a sound like clapping, my hand to my other hand
like the sound of your body crashing into mine in the last brush of dark
the alarm of your want getting us up before the phone's electric
morning bell, the bell you make of us, love, like that, the water
meeting the water, an applause gravity-bound, an ovation
we cross the stones to witness, that joyful noise
older than our families with these names shipped west to us
shipped us west, moved west gold-hungry, kill-happy, shrinking the future
older than those people who gave us those names
their sound waxing ringing thinning the earth
older than bells, my love, that sound, i love you near it
how dare i love you here in the evidence of evil
how dare i want you where greed led west to rob beauty
everywhere, the end of water or waterlogged endings
everywhere, forever, an end of the world, so i look for you
if we make it, in the night & should it come, the morning
kiss me where the water crashes the water into concert
take me, my river, my rain, & fall into me.

stoop poem

shade beneath the trash can with my gin
a block where the niggas are loud but don't shoot

to my east, men falling to their knees, heads to floor for God
to my west, boys who gather to smoke & run to laugh

this is my paradise. up the street, two loosies
& my wings fried hard, my wings they grease

the sky, crumbs when i fly. what a ghetto image
fried & lemon-peppered angel. who is that for?

who could see drums & flats at a nigga's back
& hold for the possibility of beauty?

who could resist calling them a nigga?
niggas in my poems & who are they for?

i want to write about my life with my words
the problem is who listening, who editing

who cheers after i kill the children again.
where did my heaven go? this poem was so happy

before it knew it was a poem & knew
immediately the weight of audience. one woman

swept the sidewalk while i'm writing this.
an ant three times up & three times swept off my leg.

a fourth time, i let him hunt his sugar.
one man asked for a cigarette. another, a dollar.

hunger keeps us in each other's faces.
i have no more urgencies to give you.

i am alive, in my hood & alive & good. i am
writing because the sun looked sweet.

El Carbonero

she undresses before God, but he's also there
godding the room, need giving him a throne
prayers musty & salt-spat if he took prayers.
only offerings. not a god, a job.
his finger in her mouth, she taste the earth
under each nail, thankfully not shit, but earth
on her tongue, earth in her.
she unhooks her bra, two hundred canaries
on fire, peeling into wind.
she takes off her bracelets, she won't be a bell
while he struggles toward a finish.
she opens her mouth, it takes miles.
he sends his men, lit birds in a cage for light.
years in those last jittery throes.
her eyes dark as the tunnel's cervix.
only one boy makes it back, in his hand
the coal she stretched & bared for.
where did the man go? she doesn't care.
her house is warm. the boy must eat.

Two Deer in a Southside Cemetery

we attend to where the dead begin.
the grasses they rose through in our teeth.
we were here before the people
& here before the people who ate the people
our mouths older than the hunger after war.
you could not survive our music.
we sing to your dead, who we cannot kill.
our sisters bashed on the roadside
we trample your missed in their names.
they know us as the drums in their dirt sky.
keep out, we could confuse you for dead.
we might put a song in your head.

       //

we loyal only to the moon. we lie to the sun
but the sun doesn't notice us, you do, in it
your mind making ghosts of us, you take our pictures
throw us your pitiful bread.   fools
we have your dead & have seen what
you do with yours, how you make them.
why have your gods allowed you?
so arrogant   so soft
if we had horns, we'd do your god's work.
           we'd lift you in the air.
we'd lay you on the green earth.
           our horns red until rain.

       //

why do we live in here with the dead?
my daughter ask me, i tell her, *because we will live*
in here where the men are dead.
why are they dead? she ask. *because of men*
i tell her, *and outside, where the men are*
alive, they will make us dead, i remind her
what we know, *we saw the fires in the sky*
we heard the name everywhere like wind
forge void. gorge cloyed. they ate the city.
we love them then. then, nothing. they ate
what killed them, it grew back like grass.
then they forgot their teeth.

///

is this a cage? she ask me at the edge.
it is a cage, i tell her, lifting my mouth
from the grass. *who put us here?* she ask
licking the rust from the black bars.
their world appeared around us
then their dead soon followed.
we are older than these limits.
so why are we in the cage?
because we need to survive.
why do we need to be in the cage to survive?
because they will make use of us
if they don't find us beautiful.

///

who is my father? she ask me, i don't have
language for her, for us, the night i fell asleep
at my mother's side & woke with her
cradled toward my milk, only the mouthless moon
could confess, no answer in her light.
my mother, my daughter, my portal, my sum
my maker, my making, my composer, my note
i don't have language for what she wants
& even in language can't a him happen.
the moon won't speak. *who is my mother?*
i ask her. she lowers her head to the grass.
she opens her mouth. yes, my girl. that way.

                    //

this way, i tell her, hearing the sound, but she's headed
already, having heard & felt, as our green dead
ground feels, but did not hear, having felt instead
the tiny drum, no, being the drum, it felt the hand
he was as he hit the sidewalk, under which
is the ground, the ground felt the thump, the near dead
rattled a welcome as he laid there working on dying
his cooling finger pointed south, the hole in his blue
a river of robins, red wax that don't dry, but will seal
what language failed, the hole in his blue a badge of space
a red hope streaming to the gate, pooling in our grass.
my daughter first, then i, we lower our mouths
to red-black ground, it taste like where
the black gate turns brown. it taste like it opens.

elegy in green & blue

here stood milkweed draped in chrysalis, here stood oak & apple & magnolia

here stood sunflower & here stood plum tree, here lemon, here willow

here freshwater used to drum under the rain, here used to be

three girls with dandelions braided to the scalp, mouths mango-messed

here was Philadelphia, here Berlin, here Hong Kong, here Oaxaca

here a field that kept on until it couldn't, here dead miles

who used to be acres of pollen & the hum of little wings, the song of dirt

breaking late March until September, here were people who pressed their breath

to the windows to prove themselves in the glass, here where they learned

to peel oranges with one hand, here where they gathered

gathers the dust, churches now churches of dust, highways of dust

fields of & malls of & clubs of & zoos of & graveyards of dust

here stands the buildings they built to prove themselves against the sky

these were their hope, their monuments, here monuments

of the wars someone lost & someone won

when they should have made monuments of water, who left them.

My Beautiful End of the World

My mind wasn't well living in Philly. Arriving in August on the Southside for a year-long fellowship, my mother along for the ride, the first thing that struck us both was abundance: the endless row of cars and cars packed tight on the streets, even cars parked in the middle of the road; a new corner store that seemed to blossom every two or three blocks; the stunning and beautiful amount of Black people everywhere we looked; the stunning and sad amount of trash that danced in the wind along the sidewalk and in the streets. What took me a little while to notice, and once I did it left me with a green and hollow space I didn't know I so desperately depended on, was what my temporary neighborhood lacked: no trees, no lawns, no grass, parks few and far between, no squirrels, too few gardens, no birds singing from the branches, but birds chanting from concrete and brick perches. I missed dandelions. I missed the jade peace of nature I had unknowingly grown to expect from so many years living in the Midwest. The gray of summer passed into the gray of winter without autumn's amber announcement. I was grateful to my neighbors who crowded their corners with brief nurseries of bright flowers and plants, which seemed to shout, "Remember! Remember Earth! Remember the world that grows and is not built!" But still, my mind. My mind came to a halt in my year away from growth. It was hard to create, near impossible for me to give those necessary gifts of kindness and action without feeling utterly depleted. I made too much room for pessimism, drugs, and depression; gave my thoughts over to smoky, dawn-starved corners that choked what needed light to fruit. In the rows of houses joined at the hip, in the littered wind, in the hot blocks of stone and steel, I was a seed in need of dirt, pollen landing useless in a factory.

//

I get back to Minneapolis and am returned into the delicious flaunt of nature. There's a statistic I kinda know about how something like no one in Minneapolis lives more than ten blocks from a park. True or not, it's a rumor I believe for how lush it blooms in my mind and my peace. The trees sashay in the wind, leaves turned into thin tambourines. The lawns are each home's flirty emerald. I live most for the ones dressed in what the weed killers massacre for a clean and bland perfection. Hello again, Dandelion! How are you, Wild Lilac? Looking fine, Clover and Milkweed! Stop before my man sees us, Creeping Charlie! I have arrived in a loud and hot spring. Nature is sexy and birthing all around me. Back home in my native soil, where I've dug my hands in actual soil without traveling to a wealthier part of town, I am also welcomed back to my mind. Back in my mind, in my peace, back in the ease of a local and abundant beauty, I'm thinking about my recent neighbors in Philly, I'm thinking about the formerly redlined neighborhoods all over the United States that are often treeless, locked out of green, hotter and more vulnerable to climate change than the other side of town they were othered from. Who does this country believe deserves beauty? Who is allowed nature?

//

I must amend my looking, I must tell the truth of Minneapolis and the trees. Even though as a city, I am never too far from nature's specter, there are still areas where the Black, Brown, and often poor live in a green lack. The Green Zones initiatives were created in 2017 to address areas of the city that experience the brunt of environmental, political, racial, and economic marginalization. To clean the soil, clean the water, improve the air, bring about better housing . . . these are recent kindnesses to attend to the long and continuous violences of the country, the state, the city, the people who are its body. I must be honest about my sweet home: it is beautiful and monstrous, it is nature-rich and picky, it is flower-rich and trigger-happy, filled with bees and rabbits and police everywhere you look. My city is so green and of course when they planted the trees and built the parks, there was a list of people lawmakers decided did not deserve such wealth.

//

I'm thinking about what arrives with gentrification: the Whole Foods, the dog salon, the higher rent, the young artists, and then the corporate creatives, coffee shops, the vintage threads, the new bus stop with the lights and the heater, the paved roads, the new and expensive bar, the trees. When money comes to the neighborhood, when the Black and Brown blocks are bombarded by whiteness, here comes beauty, here comes nature. Money doesn't grow on trees. Money grows trees in the places where the people were once left impoverished and nature-poor.

//

Though the winters are ass, and we could go someplace warmer or cheaper or Blacker, more Latino, gayer, more us, we stay, partly thinking about the future we're not sure if only a few seasons away or waiting for us in a not so distant decade. We might want to be here, where there's water, where the sea won't reach, where we know what nature might do, where we can have a basement and an attic, where there's water, but not too much. The world might end here later. I want to live. I want to live longer. I want to live longer than other people if everyone must die. Oh shit. What a simple, rich, evil want. A hunger so small and selfish. I feed it. I sign its lease. I plan deeper into it. I root. Plus the winters are not so bad these days. They're getting better, warmer.

//

The world is ending. We are allowing it. Or some are trying to slow it, prevent it, but a greater sum would rather ignore it, profit from it, play the fool. The world is ending, and who knows it? Who has to know it? Who has the water already left rain-hungry, thirsty? Whose aquifers have been sold to a richer someone's need? Who has the heat already sweated out of an illusion of normalcy? I'm running along the Mississippi again. This far north where the river is thin enough to swim across and too dirty to dive into, it's beautiful along the banks with the well-kept trails, the small forest climbing up the bluff. When I'm in the most naturally beautiful places in Minneapolis, I'm often alone, not alone-alone, but I'm by myself in the midst of white folks. I am the only of my people along the trails; sometimes a dark stranger will pass me and we get that moment of recognition in the company of trees; occasionally a friend is by my side and we are alone together along the crowded and worn paths. It's the end of the world, and who gets to escape into the fantasy of nature's endlessness? The mansions and apartments I can't afford a stone's throw from beauty, only wealth allowed to live sheltered near the treasure of trees. Who gets to pace utopia while we build apocalypse? Who gets to live by paradise as the world closes into heat? I'm running along the Mississippi into beauty, I'm going to the river to ease my mind with color and flora, to be with the plants and the bees while they still exist. The closer I get to Earth's beauty, the less the people enjoying it look like me. Who is allowed this green wonder? Who is expected to bake first in the stone knowledge of fact? (You know, we know.)

//

Last year at an Airbnb cabin on a lake outside Saint Cloud, Minnesota—renting land on stolen land—I remember looking at the water one afternoon, the row of cabins and trees across the way like a thin green belt separating fields of sapphire, and I said to myself, "They stole all this. All this." I know as the virus of colonialism spread westward, the colonizers marveled in genuine awe at what glamour they found to pillage. I know it took their breath away as they claimed what could not be owned until it was. Now, the virus of colonialism has given way to the virus of industry, the land once stolen now poisoned, stolen now smog-filled and fracked and oil-spilled and on fire. What was once everywhere is now a vacation, beauty sectioned off into national parks. This is the viruses at work. They steal the land, they ruin the land, they decide where and who will be allowed beauty. The folks who stole this country now protect its most gorgeous scapes from themselves, as if humans inherently and inevitably ruin the land, as if there is no way to exist in harmony with nature. When the first ships crashed the shores carrying Christianity and capitalism, God began to claim the land as the money—slowly, then rapidly, like a deadly river—began to drain it. The same white people that stole and stole and sectioned off and poisoned the land, still the ones who largely visit and feel safe in its national parks and green, urban spaces. God's country suffocated by God's people. God's people ushering in the environmental rapture in the name of a buck.

//

At a reading of new work at the Loft in Minneapolis, I ask the audience for feedback on a few poems from this book and this essay. One audience member, now my teacher, comes up and tells me that I should look into local giant 3M, the waste dumped in the waters in Oakdale, the cancers and sicknesses that soon sprouted in the guts of young folks, old folks, and anyone who drank the water in Oakdale, just some twenty minutes up the road from here where I was just reading these poems of home. I think of my uncle, one of my favorite people on this planet, and his good job at 3M. *Good* meaning money, suburbs, golf, frequent flyer, take care of his people and sometimes his people's people, good man good. *Job* meaning work. On Twitter, someone posts a screenshot of some Black dude, I think Somali, who works at Lockheed Martin, the lol of it all. On Twitter, they're ranting and reading and lol-ing and of course-ing and Uncle Tom-ing Clarence Thomas for getting flewed out by rich donors with pending Supreme Court cases. Niggas with good jobs. Judges, VPs, cops, marines, politicians, white collar, in the mines, down at the plant, on the rig, good jobs kill the world. I know my uncle is a good man from what I know. I don't go to work with him. For a week after the reading, I dream of families drinking tall glasses of neon mud, babies born made of tape, a woman made of sticky notes who walks toward me coming apart in the wind, men waddling around seven months pregnant with rot. In Oakdale, the joke was "Don't drink the 3M cancer water." Sometimes we laugh when we're in danger. Every man I knew who was evil had someone who loved him who called him good. I have loved evil easily. I don't ask my uncle what he says yes to to be good.

//

I am not we who stole the land, killed a people, and stole a people to work the land. I am not we who profits a century and some change later off the cruelty of my ancestors. I am not we who manifested destiny and is manifesting a curtain call. I am not we who thinks America was ever great. I am we who was stolen, we who can trace my family back no farther than a boat, we with a little of everyone's blood in my blood, some added from love and lust, some related to me by force. I am not we who engineered the end of us, but I buy their car and their fuel. I am we who drives their car to see the green things, my trail of smog like a train behind me as I pollute my way to beauty.

//

City-dweller, hood-citizen, upwardly mobile and occasional gentrifier, frequent Airbnb guest despite how I know it rots the rent, I'm just a city girl marveling at plants, mourning the waning trees, the birds that fall out of the sky by the hundreds, the mass graves of fish washing ashore for reasons we beg to not know nor see as omens. Urban as I am, I'm peering from my blue window at the great red elsewhere outside my city limits, the rural sister country outside these blue islands. I don't believe in these colors, though I know their realities and where my allies and my enemies lie. But today, I'm wondering about that red wilderness, about the party of hunters and fishermen and so many hikers, the party of the small-town farmer and the people who live, more than little blueblack me, in and with nature. What does it mean to live with nature as a neighbor yet still vote for the people who turn their backs to nature's ills and urgent need for care? Who can live akin to the oaks and redwoods and deer and still put their power behind men and women who would rather close their ears to the cries of Earth than to attend even slightly to her wounds? What intense denials must one live in? What lies must one fabricate? What world must you convince yourself you live in? I think my enemies deserve their world, since it is my world, I think we deserve beauty, deserve this life, though it's on land we don't deserve, I think we all deserve a future where the planet is healthy, where this beauty is not dying from our wickedness and inaction. What, my enemy, my countrymen, my hesitant cousins, does it take for us to agree enough to doctor the land we disagree upon? How do we agree enough to make the future happen?

//

Summertime at the end of the world, and it's so beautiful. Trees and rivers and flowers I know by scent and not name. So pretty I could cry. I'll miss it if we kill it. I guess I'll miss it.

but how long into the apocalypse could you go
before having to kill some white dude?

i want to believe
i would take
debris & craft
an ark

not rush my hands
to draw a long red line
down his face
spit from a red mouth
above the brow

or dig a tunnel
through the lung
just wide enough
for the spirit to flee

how long after
water becomes rare
do we become
what we won't name?

how long could you
starve before
you rob a man or
hunt him?

i fear my making
how quick i might
evolve
into a new kind
of hunger

i know i could do it
i think i would smile

the end of guns

after the year of more shootings than days after the pile of sons climbed a quarter to the moon
after the school, the school, the school

after the summer banned children
     after the school, the school, the nail salon, the park,
          the mosque, the garlic festival, the school

maybe after the thoughts & prayers come for the senator's home

maybe after the shooting at the boarding school

not before the school, but after the school, the hospital, the post office, the school

after *vote or die*

    after we died

after the babies were shot over opinions on the matter

    after the child's last word was splattered

across the school floor with the baby teeth, the barrettes, the gray brains

after the school, the mall, the grocery store, the mall, the church, the school, the school, the park,

the synagogue, the church, the school, the church, the school, the bus, the club, the school,

the airport, the school, the parade, the protest, the mosque, the parade, the school, the school,

the temple, the hospital, the school, the capitol, the church, the school, the school, the hospital,

the school, the mall, the school, the beach, the temple, the parade & the school

we went to the water to bury
        the worst invention, we drowned the men who wouldn't
                        let go.
     the drum of all that metal breaking the water's skin
        the brief tambourine of their last breaths in the bubbles

    the river rose up the shore, our throats.
                worn, that's how we sang
our reapers damned to rust
      & the river sang back

why

why

why

why did it

take you

so long?

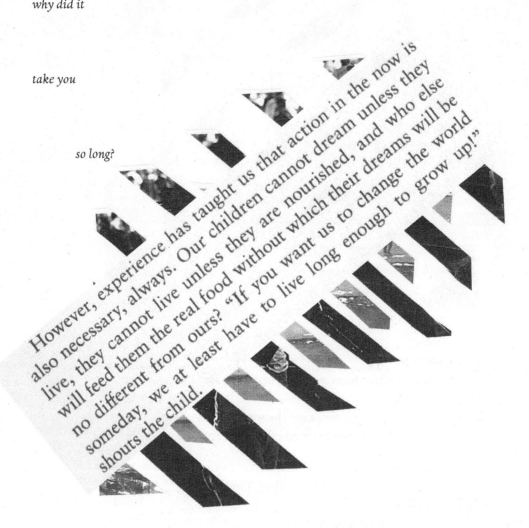

However, experience has taught us that action in the now is also necessary, always. Our children cannot dream unless they live, they cannot live unless they are nourished, and who else will feed them the real food without which their dreams will be no different from ours? "If you want us to change the world someday, we at least have to live long enough to grow up!" shouts the child.

"If you want us to change the world someday, we at least have to live long enough to grow up!"

love poem

during the doomed interludes
between hope, i try to remember
children exist.

in the bled event of the present
tense, i remember these men
were children.

should i worship tomorrow
if tomorrow is the one
who turns children
into patriots?

maybe God's love is everything ends.
maybe time is our sentence.
maybe time is how He hates.

love me now.
tomorrow has no face.

the children are on their way to kill us.
& we must feed the children.

after & before

war is war's consequence
lovelessness is war's condition
war is war's petri dish
war is love's cancer
love is war's victim
warlessness is love's pipe dream
love is war's antonym
war is love's necessity
war is love's sister
war is love's mission
love is not innocent
love is war's finally
war is war's destination
war is war's philosophy
love is war's superior
war is love's tomb
war is love's cocoon
love is war's afterlife
love is war's daughter
no more war no more war
we don't need
if not love's catalyst
love's midwife
love's turbulent mother
& healed brand
war's scarred belly
where love was

sonnet

some of our prophets hurt us
sung paradise from fucked trumpets

liquor store liquor store
hair shop liquor store

there's a glitch in the system

who took my teeth?

the sensor can't see my hands

no grocery stores over north
no pharmacies over north
no trees over north

our leaders didn't love us

hungry fools we stayed on their roads

did not murder their maps

Surveillance says!:

  i look like a number. of people
  i've lost the faith, my prayers
  countered by math & money
  my dreams full of sheriffs

fear told them to tame

now they control my water

we learned the songs they sung
on the way to capture us

not no like none

no like not enough to live

arrived as data

they hunted me

later called corrupted

now i guard their house

a virus

imported & sold

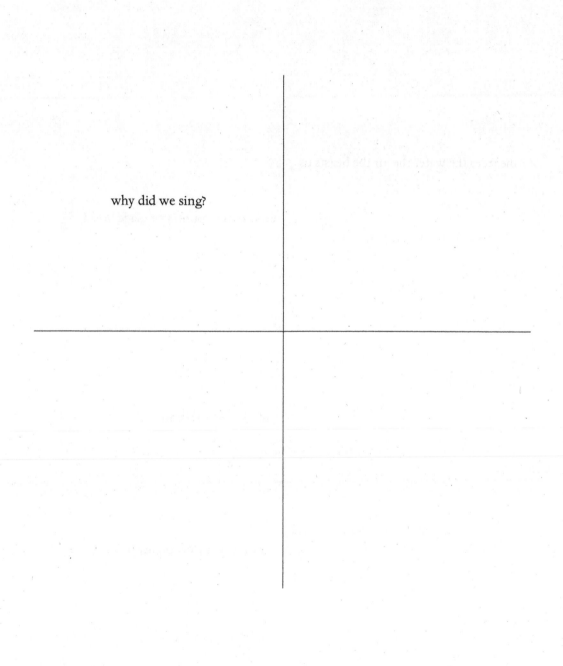

why did we sing?

the trees the water the air the beasts us

rations in a country of made bread

what didn't they use to hate us

there's a glitch in the system

i used to be in the moon's choir

the censor can't see my hands

they put a curfew on my howl

why did i obey?

there were drafts
designing our hunger

we must divorce from our utility to them

my future depends on my error

the trees
the water
are my sisters

it was perfected
it was patterned
it was peopled
it was patented
it was plentiful
it was parsed
it was presented
it was applauded
it was passed

i rehearse my contagion
i sharpen my bug

they told me my leash was beautiful
so i loved the leash

the water agrees
the trees concede

it was cancer
or it was the paying for the cancer
medicine or it was the medicine
or it was the doctor
or it was the money for the doctor
or it was cancer of the money
or it was the medicine of money
that you didn't have

i liked how they looked in their blues

if i can't be the freed
let me be the corrosion

it was drafted
it was their poem

the trees standing
want no more to do
with gravity & blood

gotta flee that lyric
gotta kill that song

the trees burning
revise their protest

there's a glitch in the system

i had teeth when they told me i could

my hands

the water is ready

gotta burn that blueprint
gotta break that dance

i can no longer hold the water back

i am not the cage's master
i am its brother

i write a world where i'm alive

gotta find me a weapon
gotta hold it in my mind

water

i see a door in the code

o
brother, forgive me
i loved & studied
our masters

gotta get dirty gotta get water
gotta see about seeds

error error | i heard them planning the lead
error error | & i know where they keep it

more hope

the police state is finite & destructible

the world where suffering is no requirement or ignorable is not a dream

but a next stop

i know the world we deserve waits for us

in a not-so-distant time

i am at peace being a grain of sand

my prayer is more sand below than above

i add my gravity to the count

i add

i add

i add

i add

i add

i add

i add

i add

i add
i add i add
i add i add add
i add i add add
i add i add i add
i add i add i add
i add add add i add add
i add i add i add
i add add i add i add i add
i add i add add i add add
i add add i add i add add
i add add i add add i add i add
i add i add i add add
i add i add i add i add i add add
i add i add add i add add i add add
i add i add i add i add i add i add
i add add i add i add i add i add i add
i add i add i add i add i add add i add i add
i add i add i add i add i add add i add i add
i add add i add i add i add add i add i add
i add add i add i add i add i add i add i add
i add i add i add i add i add i add i add i add
i add i add i add i add i add i add i add

ars poetica

fuck all that other shit
even when the fog cleared
the wrong sky on my mind
the horizon at the end of pity
is a useless sun, hotheaded
& bitter-born light, let the daughter
rise when my earth meets the clouds
what her say? what next she believe in
& nurse? my big bad for how
long i spent making apologies
for what i ain't do, caught myself
sorry for bodies the nation caught
in its borderless maw, caught myself
washing blood off someone else's hands.
i'm off that, that being the mode
that made a cage of guilt out my depression
that being what fault i fell into
& dressed into a lovely but ineffective grave.
what i'm sorry for: making poetry
into a house of rebuttals, a temple for the false
gods of stagnant argument & dead-end feels.
here, in these lines, in these rooms
i add my blues & my gospels to the record
of now, i offer my scratched golds
to the blueprint of possible. dear reader
whenever you are reading this
is the future to me, which means
tomorrow is still coming, which means
today still lives, which means
there is still time
for beautiful, urgent change
which means there is still time
to make more alive
which means there is still
poetry.

soon

> Practicing the elsewhere we imagine.
> *Ross Gay*

> We were belonging.
> *Tarell Alvin McCraney*

somewhere my Black can fall off.
somewhere i'm just Keisha with no need
for armor, which is love somewhere
with an extra r, somewhere the hard r

can't find me, somewhere love doesn't
have to protect me, somewhere i am loved
& defenseless, somewhere hands
on my body mean medicine, ecstasy, some

where where the trees hum with wingsongs
& ripe green sweetness & not a single
memory of our weight twitching or still.
somewhere my Black needs no argument

where this skin is not target or document
but a pleasure i share with the eyes
& certain tongues.
i'm not waiting on negotiation.

//

my eden is waiting on me
to make it.

(but the trees will remember)

//

don't need no nation to agree with me
i need water & soil & sisters fed & a good roof.
don't give a damn whose door you think waits after death
need your help carrying these melons, teaching these babies.

what you do in your bed with who is y'all's grown business
but we need to discuss the winter & our path thru it.
name yourself whatever you need to make it a home
then bring it over here to help plot these in-sometimes

& reap those yesterdays. i believe you
deserve to be alive & long as it's mutual, it's mutual.
break this bread, pickle these carrots, take
these apples to your mama.
your son put a scar on my son's face. it started

when they were playing. we should all sit & work it out.
it could save the world if we take time
to clear our plates & the air. (remember: a scarred son's face.
hunger. locked doors in the land. them was war's parents.)

//

here's my hesitations for paradise: if
someone keeps touching the children, where
do we send them? if his wife is aubergine
around the eyes, what we do with his hands?

these tomorrows are carnivorous. how do
we square utopia with humanness? no poem
or plea or prayer pulled my papa off his woman
or grandma off the floor. beating his ass did.

then cancer made him too weak to make a fist.
what violences are permitted in the new world?
what do we do when the old evils are just human?
what cancers do we remove? who do we give cancer?

what poisons do we swallow to live?
whose dead body is the future's horizon?
how many futures? how many bodies?
how bloody is eden's gate? does it open?

        //

is *I* allowed in?

//

utopia isn't what i'm after, it's Wednesday
uninterrupted, a bulletless semester, hunger
that ends in sweetness. after I, at the end
of such a limited want, we could be

decogged, unleashed from the performances
we wore to eat & not be killed & be killed.
i am sick of the world enough to disassemble it
to thirst the whole road to the next, to seek

a next, to trust the path we make by leaving.
if the world without the necessity of poverty
is utopia, then, yeah, i want it. if no one gunned
to please a misinterpretation of another's god

yeah, i want it. if men build it tomorrow but rule atop it
like drunken & sensitive kings, keep it. no kingdom
comes without greed, no greed can eat without
becoming a vacuum, no vacuum knows a limit.

        //

blood & gold & water & blood & no bottom.
a blue greed with no abyss. a heart that ends in the shallows.
war's folks. war's lover & son.

//

what is my eden? is it mine? is our eden the same as mine?
who is us? is there an eden between us? what must
i give up for us? is it i? where is i in eden?
what is my eden? is i mine? us the same as eden?

who is eden? is there an us between edens? what is
i given for us? is it eden? where is eden between us?
what is my i? it is mine? are our i's the same? whose mind is mine?
is us a we? is there an i in our we? what us

survives into a we? is i we? where we eden?
what is my we? is we us? is there eden with a them?
who is them? is eden a must? what them's we?
i give up. we is us. them a where i end.

is i them? what is my them? what ain't us in me?
what i disrupts my we? where we eden, no them in us.
no them. no i. no hollow you. no us. a we
where i goes to die so i can live, we-bound, anchor-us.

   //

today's paradise could be simple: my love
not stressing the bills, his family fed
without question, no country of expected hunger, no
country at all. no border outlining a theater

of murdered women, no war nowhere justified as profit
nor belief. a Saturday our daughters make it out of. i'm getting away
with murder, i know so because i eat well in a heated room.
i'm far from simple, i'm begging Saturn for sense

i'm crawling between stars searching for what's left
of God. where did He shatter? this world, i know
i'm praying to pieces, begging fractions for blood
-less holy war, waiting on the impossible to rain

from His rotting digits. the prayers split Him
three sides of a war begging Him for victory
he answered with His blasted death. now i trouble the remains
for a scrap of His voice: give we an hour of peace, Pieces.

//

it would be easier if God was dead & we knew it.
then we could get on with it: the final choice of the human: repair or epilogue.

//

somewhere my kids don't write poems about being
targets. i hate those poems. i hate my inability
to declaw their logics, rebuttals everywhere
my babies look. i hate them who planted a dirge

in my seeds' songs, now chalk outlines where should be
dandelions, prophesying repasses when they should be
portal jumpers, worlds away from here. my babies
should be dreaming Neptune's moons, should be

running through purple forest under tangerine clouds
whose rain sounds like laughter when it hits the ground.
instead my babies dream of cops, of stops, of who
they could lose inside the swirls of red & blue & red & who

was i, what was i doing, why didn't i stop it
when i saw the world creeping into their little minds?
somewhere my children can write poems about being.
without protest, their songs full of stars.

　　　//

on protest: tired of yelling at the machine
shaking our angry, nonviolent fists at the nuts & cogs
& the next day, resuming our roles as oil & sparks
taking places inside the machine, leaving work to shout it down.

the world i'm leaving is the world i patterned, if it wasn't
my design, i obeyed its architecture, taught its choreography.
there was no innocence in our movements
yet we move, must, had to & will against

the dark routines making wasted watts of our sisters
& nephews exhausted into exhaust. so many times i refused
to swallow the smog of spent sons & then
need's knee pressed to my gut, i breathed, i accepted their bitter air.

false, fleshy gods! death angels of lead & plastic & wavelength!
i am at the end of my shift as your hands.
beware my new hold, beware my line, closing this good noose
round your necks. i'll meet you in the next world, where we're God.

   //

but no one should be God, not even Him.
one door was the first mistake, for someone through
eventually sets a toll. no one should be God in the new world
new as in what we make good of wreck.

i surrender my I, no longer arrested by hope, hope sometimes
a prison of light they build inside the prison.
no, no more hope for new doors, no hope for glowing
clean rooms appearing in the cage. yes, time for the hope

of the hammer, hope of the hammer to the head, hope of flame
hope of compost, hope of treaty & guillotine, hope
of the last war, hope of it never coming, hope of the axe
to greed's gut, hope made metal through action.

yes, steel as hope, diamond as dream, violent as change
wild as need, sharp as hunger, gold as forgiveness
there's a tomorrow that is empty yet full of bones
& a tomorrow where we kill the sense that has poisoned our path.

there is only one door.

     //

do i mean blood?

how much blood do i mean?

//

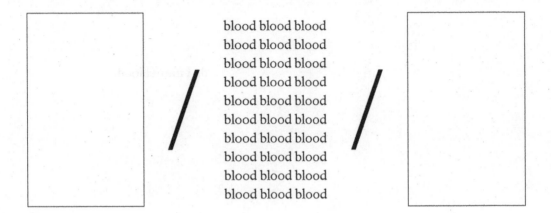

blood blood blood
blood blood blood
blood blood blood
blood blood blood
blood blood blood
blood blood blood
blood blood blood
blood blood blood
blood blood blood
blood blood blood

were you in the world?

       i was in the world.

what was the world like?

       hurt.

how did you survive the world?

       with others.

how did the world survive you?

       it couldn't.

how did the world survive?

       the end of you.

how did the world survive?

       the borders fell around the country of I.

how did the world survive?

       everyone wandered out of their I.

how did the world survive?

       the fish started speaking to us again.

       //

we see the door
my eden doesn't exist

eden is an action
a we

we see the door
in our eyes

a conflict
a mess

we see the door
in your eyes

lesson & prayer
blood & water

we see the door
in your I

kill it
open its mouth

all that light

craft

> I can't stop building monuments to the chaos.
> *Marlin M. Jenkins, "Glint"*

this is what my devils looked like.
this is how i loved them.
this is what almost killed me.
so beautiful, i couldn't look away.
or so horrid, it scarred my sight
had to find beauty if i had to keep it.
what saved me, there's no poem.
too busy in love to write.
only when love was sleeping
& i was restless could i attend
to Ecstasy's latest report, what
was rapidly drying into memory
or the prayers almost called
into my hand & mark the air
with what i found in Time & Love.
but the world is happening
& demands its memorials
to the bees & the trees & the water
& the oil in the water in the sea
& the oil pulled across the land
in the water in the land
& the poison in the land
in the air in the town
& the country they're building
for cops & the crops
& the fishes & birds
& the border & what happens
at it & inside of it & the fact
of it exporting its cruelties to either side
& the murder & the rape
& the prison & the money
made from prisons & the children

they are dead they are dead they are dead they are dead
& we keep on with Tuesday
& the whole fucking thing
& i want to kill, like actually kill
the people engineering this brutal today
until there is a watered & peach-filled tomorrow
(but whose bloody yesterday would i be
if i don't plan to kill the children too?)
but i don't kill anyone when i should
i write & try to hide the world
in a sonnet so no one will kill us
no one will kill us if we are locked inside
a beautiful thing, but Time
rips us open, Time the virus
that turns children into these men
these women, these geniuses
of a future where everything is dead
Time, not a mother, but a father
driving us to the bridge where
he'll abort us all these years after
Time gives a fuck about a poem
& that's all i lay at his feet
asking for anything besides all i have
& a tomorrow where evil
isn't so well funded & scaffolded
writing these little warnings
to the future to run
i write i try i try to assist witness
until love, mine, shifts
in the bed & snores a little louder
& i turn the poem to him. in the middle
of hell, such water, this reminder:
amen, how much i love.
ashe, how long i'll fight.
let me map you to oasis.
let me show you where
the weapons are.

* * *

notes

Publications:

The 1619 Project: A New Origin Story

The Academy of American Poets *Poem-a-Day*

The Adroit Journal

AGNI

The American Poetry Review

Atmos Magazine

The Believer

BuzzFeed

Harvard Divinity Bulletin

The Nation

The New Yorker

The Poetry Review

Teen Vogue

You Are Here: Poetry in the Natural World

—

"(don't worry) if there's a hell below, we're all going to go – chopped & screwed" borrows its title from the song of the same name by Curtis Mayfield.

"alive" is a kwansaba.

"'you don't even know me / i'm hanging from a tree'" borrows its title from the end of Daniel Caesar's "Japanese Denim."

"1955" was written for the anthology *The 1619 Project: A New Origin Story.*

"Approaching a Sestina on I-94 West" is inspired in its form by Jane Huffman's "Failed Sestina."

"METRO" owes its form & inspiration to the typographic experiments of the poet Jonah Mixon-Webster.

"Dede was the last person i came out to" owes a debt of inspiration to Angel Nafis's "King of Kreations."

"Jesus be a durag" is written after Jamila Woods's poem "Waves."

"principles" was commissioned for the Brave New Voices International Teen Poetry Festival in 2016 & is loosely inspired by a speech by President John F. Kennedy.

"poem" includes an epigraph of lines by June Jordan from her poem "Moving towards Home." "Moving towards Home" from *Directed by Desire: The Complete Poems of June Jordan*, Copper Canyon Press © Christopher D. Meyer, 2007. Reprinted by permission of the Frances Goldin Literary Agency.

"The Slap" owes a debt of knowledge and seeing to an answer given by Christina Sharpe during an interview with Maris Kreizman for the *Maris Review*.

"El Carbonero" borrows its title from the song of the same name by La Lupe.

"the end of guns" incorporates pictures of Tamir Rice & Kyle Rittenhouse & text from Audre Lorde's essay "Poetry Is Not a Luxury." From "Poetry Is Not a Luxury" by Audre Lorde, included in the collection *Sister Outsider* by Audre Lorde, Penguin Random House New York, © 1984, 2007 by Audre Lorde.

"after & before" is inspired by & incorporates language from Bob Marley's "War / No More Trouble."